684

The Upside-Down Man

The Upside-Down Man

RUSSELL BAKER

ILLUSTRATED BY GAHAN WILSON

McGraw-Hill Book Company

NEW YORK   ST. LOUIS   SAN FRANCISCO   MONTREAL   TORONTO

Library of Congress Cataloging in Publication Data

Baker, Russell, date.
The upside-down man.
Summary: A mad scientist and a boy who can't
do anything right team up to make a man.
I. Wilson, Gahan. II. Title.
PZ7.B17498Up [Fic] 77-6272
ISBN 0-07-003356-0   ISBN 0-07-003357-9 lib. bdg.

12345 RAHO 78987

In THE FARAWAY KINGDOM of Delirium, where the days were always dark and the nights were filled with thunder and lightning, there lived a mad scientist. His name was Doctor Frankenstein.

One day that was darker than most Doctor Frankenstein arrived in the mountain village of Skar.

He saw that the clouds which always hung over the village were dark purple and black and blue—even at noontime—and he liked that.

1

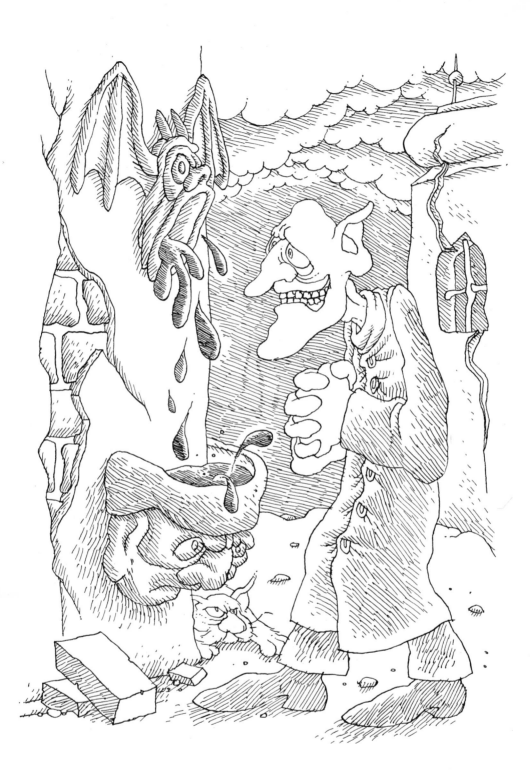

He saw that the fish in the stream which ran past the village were dying, and he liked that, too.

He saw that the water which splashed in the village fountain was brown with dirt, and that also pleased him.

He listened carefully to the trees but did not hear a single nightingale singing, or even a blue jay squawking, or, for that matter, not even a sparrow twittering in the air, and all that made him like the village of Skar very much.

"This looks like just the place for my kind of work," Doctor Frankenstein said. And he walked into the village inn where at that very moment the innkeeper was busy beating a boy with a broom.

"You bumbler!" the innkeeper cried as the broom whacked the boy's ears. "I told you to throw out the dishwater. The dishwater! Not the dishes!"

"I'm sorry!" cried the boy, holding his arm up to save his head from the innkeeper's broom. "I thought you said, 'Throw out the dishes.' "

This made the innkeeper beat him harder than before.

"You bumbler!" he shouted. "You have smashed seven of my best plates!"

A crowd of people watched the beating with pleasure. The people of Skar did not like bumblers, even when the bumblers were just boys.

"The innkeeper should beat him with the iron fireplace poker instead of the broom," one said.

"The innkeeper should send him to jail," said another.

"Lazlo!" the innkeeper shouted, for Lazlo was the boy's name. "Lazlo, you are fired! Fired! No more work! Understand?"

Doctor Frankenstein paid no attention to this scene as he walked into the inn. Being a mad scientist, he did not notice everyday things. He was far too busy having great ideas and dreaming of the day when he would be known as the greatest mad scientist in the whole kingdom of Delirium.

"Would you please stop sweeping that boy long enough to give me some advice?" Doctor Frankenstein asked the innkeeper.

"I am Doctor Frankenstein, a mad scientist, and I wish to settle near this fine village."

When the people heard this, they lost interest in beating Lazlo, for mad scientists were great heroes in the kingdom of Delirium.

King Zugg the Third, the ruler of Delirium, had ordered all his subjects to respect mad scientists, and take good care of them, and make sure they did not catch pneumonia. Without its mad scientists, the King had said, Delirium would not be able to make the new guns and bombs needed to save itself from the dreadful kingdom of Isteria.

Since no mad scientist had ever before come to Skar, the innkeeper and the villagers were so excited they let Lazlo crawl away while they crowded around Doctor Frankenstein.

To do his work, the Doctor said, he needed a spooky castle at the edge of a dark mountain. It would have to have many, many cobwebs, he said, and high towers which were easily hit by lightning.

"There is just such a castle at the edge of Doom Mountain," said the innkeeper.

"Does it have plenty of trapdoors?" asked Doctor Frankenstein.

"Hundreds of trapdoors," replied one of the villagers. "Or so people say. Nobody now alive in the village has ever set foot inside that terrible place."

"How about dungeons?" asked Doctor Frankenstein.

"The dungeons are awful, Doctor," said an old woman. "I have heard my grandmother say they are bottomless and filled with huge spiders."

"Very, very good," said Doctor Frankenstein, "but is there a big workroom with a floor that can open suddenly at the touch of a button and drop everyone standing on it down into endless inky-black night?"

"My great-grandfather once told me there is such a

5

room," said the innkeeper. "He said you could push a red button and drop all your enemies down into a yawning pit too horrible to think about."

Thinking about it, all the villagers shivered.

"I shall go there and look," said Doctor Frankenstein, walking to the door. There he turned back to the villagers.

"A warning to you all," he said. "You are forbidden ever to talk about my visit to anyone. Not to your children. Not to your friends."

"Not even to our wives?" asked the innkeeper.

"To no one," said Doctor Frankenstein. And then he smiled. "Remember those dungeons," he warned. "And the big spiders." And he walked out.

"Whew!" said all the villagers.

"This must be top secret!" said one.

"He must be on a secret mad scientific project for King Zugg," said another.

"Shhhh!" said the innkeeper.

L AZLO SAT by the stream which ran past the village and dabbed water on his bruises. He was thirsty, but did not dare drink from the stream, for everyone said its water killed people as well as fish.

He wondered what in the world he would do now. Since his parents were dead, he lived in an orphanage which was run by three very serious men.

"If you don't learn to stop bumbling, Lazlo," the three very serious men had told him, "we shall send you to King Zugg's army. And believe us, once you are in King Zugg's army you will learn to stop bumbling—or else!"

"Or else what?" Lazlo had asked.

"In King Zugg's army," the three very serious men had said, "all bumblers are dipped slowly into tanks of boiling oil."

Lazlo was certain he would never learn to stop bumbling, even in King Zugg's army. *Maybe some people are born to be bumblers,* Lazlo thought. The world must certainly need bumblers or there would not be so many of us. Lazlo felt sorry for himself. Were bumblers really such bad people? he wondered.

"A bumbler," he said, "is just a person who cannot do anything right when he tries to help people. And he usually hurts himself even more than he hurts others.

"Take me," Lazlo said. He was talking out loud to himself now, not seeing that a man was walking toward him. "When I get the innkeeper's orders wrong he loses seven plates, but I get a beating. When I fry an egg, I break the yolk. When I drive a nail, I mash my finger with the hammer."

"Isn't that beautiful!" cried the man who had come up behind Lazlo. He pointed to the stream.

The voice startled Lazlo. It belonged to Doctor Frankenstein.

"What is beautiful?" Lazlo asked.

"The way those fish are dying there in the stream," said the Doctor. "You seem the only boy in this village with enough love of beauty to come out here and watch. I'll bet you will make a good mad scientist one of these days. How would you like to work for me?"

Lazlo asked what kind of work Doctor Frankenstein had in mind.

"I am going to make a man," said the Doctor, "and I

need an assistant who knows how people are put together. Have you ever put anybody together before?"

Lazlo said he had never put anybody together and did not think he would be good at it.

"Whenever I fry an egg," he said, "I break the yolk. Whenever I drive a nail, I mash my fingers with the hammer." He showed Doctor Frankenstein his fingers, which were badly mashed.

"In that case," Doctor Frankenstein said, "you should be just right for the job, since it will not require you either to fry eggs or drive nails."

That was how Lazlo came to be Doctor Frankenstein's assistant.

The two of them went to the spooky castle at the edge of Doom Mountain, which turned out to have all the things inside that a mad scientist could hope for.

"Why do you want a spooky castle with cobwebs and trapdoors, and dungeons with spiders, and this workroom floor which can open at the push of a red button and drop everybody into an inky-black pit?" Lazlo asked one day.

Doctor Frankenstein explained that these things discouraged visitors from dropping in at the castle.

"Making a man is very complicated work," he said. "We would never get the job done if visitors were always coming by to stare at us."

Doctor Frankenstein and Lazlo worked night and day

for many weeks. By Halloween the job was almost finished. All Doctor Frankenstein needed was a wild thunderstorm with lightning brilliant enough to shake the mountain.

"I don't like lightning," Lazlo grumbled.

"Without the lightning," Doctor Frankenstein said, "I cannot bring the man to life."

He showed Lazlo how big metal bolts on the sides of the man's head were connected to wires. These wires would lead the lightning into the man and bring him to life.

"It will be just like turning on a light bulb," Doctor Frankenstein explained.

That night the worst thunderstorm anyone could remember hit Doom Mountain. Thunder shook the stones of the castle and lightning danced in the forest.

While Lazlo huddled in a corner of the workroom wishing he had gone into King Zugg's army instead of working for a mad scientist, lightning struck the wires connected to the bolts in the head of Doctor Frankenstein's man.

Smoke came from the man's nose.

Sparks flew from his ears.

The bolts in the sides of his head glowed red hot.

Then all the lights in the castle went out. It was as dark as the inside of a pyramid at midnight.

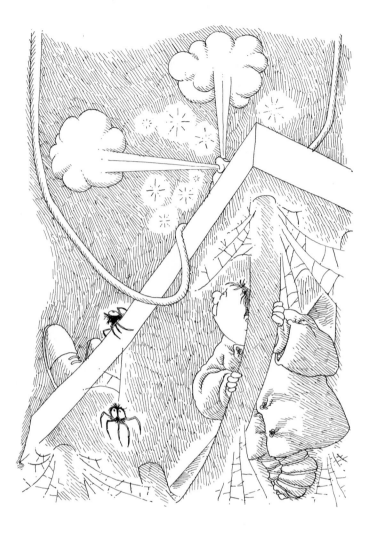

"I'll get a candle," said Lazlo.

"Don't you dare move!" Doctor Frankenstein shouted. "In this dark you might accidentally touch the red button that would open the floor and drop us down into the inky-black pit."

Lazlo sat still and let Doctor Frankenstein get the candle. The Doctor lit it.

"Look!" shouted Lazlo, pointing to the table.

The candle's flickering light showed the newly made man sitting on the edge of the table.

He blinked at Doctor Frankenstein and then at Lazlo.

"Welcome to Castle Frankenstein," the Doctor said to the brand-new man.

The brand-new man said nothing, but he looked again at Doctor Frankenstein and smiled.

Then he looked at Lazlo and smiled even more happily.

Lazlo was surprised. It was such a pleasant looking man. In the village he had never seen anyone who smiled except when they were watching someone getting a beating.

This was such a pleasant looking man! Lazlo smiled back at him because he felt good about having helped to make such a nice looking person. Maybe he had finally learned to quit bumbling. "He really looks glad to be alive," said Lazlo. Doctor Frankenstein came nearer to the new man. "How are you feeling?" asked the mad scientist.

"Moo," said the man.

"I didn't understand," Doctor Frankenstein said.

"Moo," said the man.

"What I asked you," Doctor Frankenstein explained, "was, how do you feel?"

14

"Moo," said the man. "Moo, moo."

It was obvious what had happened. Lazlo had been given the job of putting in the man's voice. And Lazlo had bumbled.

"Lazlo," said Doctor Frankenstein, "that is the dumbest piece of bumbling I have ever seen."

"What did I do wrong?" the boy asked.

"I told you to put in a loud voice," the Doctor said. "Instead, you have put in a cow voice."

"You should have spoken more clearly," said Lazlo. "I didn't think you said 'a loud voice.' I thought you said 'a cow voice.' "

"Why would I have wanted a cow's voice put in a man?" Doctor Frankenstein asked.

"It just seemed like something a mad scientist might naturally do," said Lazlo.

"Moo, moo," said the man who talked like a cow. He sounded upset.

"Well, he will just have to get used to it," the Doctor said.

Suddenly the man jumped from the table.

And—the strangest thing!

He was standing upside down!

Yes, upside down!

And yet, although he was upside down, with his head

pointed down toward the floor and his legs sticking up in the air, he was still standing on two feet.

"Lazlo," Doctor Frankenstein said, "this is the worst bumbling yet. You have put the feet in the wrong place."

The poor man no longer smiled. He was mooing sadly now, as if wondering why the world was all upside down.

"You have put his feet on the ends of his arms instead of putting them on the ends of his legs, Lazlo," Doctor Frankenstein said.

"How was I supposed to know where you wanted the feet to go?" asked Lazlo.

"Let's just see what is inside those shoes," Doctor Frankenstein said, reaching for the shoes which stuck up in the air higher than the Doctor's ears.

"Just as I suspected," he said, removing the shoes and looking angrily at Lazlo. "Hands! You have attached his hands to his ankles."

"Moo! Moo! Moo! Moo! Moo!" cried the upside-down man. He seemed to realize that something was wrong.

Swinging his right leg through the air, he grabbed the candle from Doctor Frankenstein and walked to a mirror and stared.

He stared first at himself, and then at Lazlo and Doctor Frankenstein, and then back at himself, and then at Lazlo again.

While this went on before the mirror, Doctor Frankenstein began to laugh. "I have to admit," he told Lazlo, "that he is the funniest looking man I have ever seen."

And he laughed louder and louder. Lazlo began to laugh, too. *Yes,* he thought, *it was certainly the silliest looking man ever seen in the kingdom of Delirium.*

Lazlo laughed even louder than the doctor.

"I would rather be a bumbler," he said between laughs, "than look as silly as this ridiculous upside-down man."

Doctor Frankenstein and Lazlo threw their arms around each other and laughed so hard that the lights in the castle came back on.

The poor upside-down man still stood in front of the mirror. He did not move. Tears ran out of his eyes and down over his forehead and down into his hair.

"Why do you think he is unhappy?" asked Lazlo.

"He is unhappy because he must go through life mooing like a cow," said Doctor Frankenstein.

"And because his feet are located at the ends of his arms.

"And because his hands stick straight up in the air on the ends of his legs.

"He is unhappy because you, Lazlo, have bumbled."

Lazlo said that was unfair of the Doctor.

"I admit I messed up a few parts," he said. "But I didn't do anything as bad as leaving those awful metal bolts sticking out of the sides of his head. You did that."

Doctor Frankenstein admitted the bolts in the head did make the upside-down man look different.

"Different!" said Lazlo. "Do you think any girl will ever want to go out with a man who has bolts sticking out of his head?"

With a fierce mooing, the upside-down man ran at Doctor Frankenstein and punched him in the jaw with his knee. Then he bit Lazlo on the ankle and, before they could stop him, ran out of the castle, along the edge of Doom Mountain, across the stream where the fish were dying and into the village of Skar.

When the villagers who were at the inn eating dinner saw him staring at them upside down and waving his legs in the air, they screamed and ran home to get their dogs.

Nobody in Skar had ever seen a mooing upside-down man with bolts in his head, and they did not want anyone who looked that different walking around their village.

Soon the night was filled with the yelping of dogs and the banging of guns.

Running ahead of the terrified villagers, the terrified upside-down man mooed as loudly as he could, but no one seemed to understand him, for each moo made them chase him with more fury than ever.

Deep in the forest the upside-down man finally tripped over a vine and fell against a great elm tree. He was out of breath and mooing for mercy when the pack of villagers surrounded him with a ring of flaming torches and fierce dogs.

"Kill him!" screamed a man with a fat barrel of a stomach and long rickety legs thin as beanpoles and a huge wrinkled nose that was as red as a tomato and almost as big.

"We don't want funny-looking people in Skar!" he shouted. "Everybody knows funny looking people are dangerous. We must kill him before he comes back and kills us all in our beds!"

"Yes, kill him!" the crowd shouted. "Kill him now!"

The upside-down man hid his head between his feet and mooed just as pitifully as he possibly could, and waited for the crowd to tear him to pieces.

They would have, too, and that would have been the end of the upside-down man if King Zugg the Third had not just at that moment come galloping up on his great black horse.

"What is this!" cried the King in his awful royal voice.

"I take my army on war games in the forest and find

that my subjects have caught a real enemy while my army merely plays at war."

The villagers fell back and bowed before the King.

"This is not a real enemy we have captured, your Majesty," said the innkeeper, "but something even worse. It is a man who looks dangerously different from anyone else in Delirium and who, therefore, might kill us all in our beds unless we kill him first."

"Are you sure he is not a spy from Isteria trying to steal our secrets?" asked King Zugg.

"He is too funny looking to be a spy, your Majesty," said the innkeeper. "A spy must be someone nobody will notice. This is the silliest looking creature you have ever seen in your life. It is an upside-down man."

King Zugg looked closely, and then laughed and laughed.

While he laughed, he was joined by the officers of his army—generals and colonels and majors and captains and lieutenants and master-sergeants.

All rode up on their horses, which were only half the size of King Zugg's horse. When they saw the King laughing they immediately laughed, too. Of course, they were careful not to laugh nearly as loudly as the King.

"Why does he moo like a cow?" asked the King.

"Because he is not civilized like us, your Majesty," said the innkeeper. "May we kill him now?"

"If you do," said King Zugg, "I shall wipe your village from the face of the earth. Return to your homes at once, and go to bed."

The King then told his generals he wanted the upside-down man locked in a cage and taken to the King's camp for study by the royal science advisor.

The generals gave the order to the colonels, who gave it to the majors, who gave it to the captains, who gave it to the lieutenants, who gave it to the master-sergeants, who found two soldiers who did the job.

When the generals asked why the King wanted a dangerous upside-down man in his camp, the King laughed. *It is good to have generals*, he thought.

Being King would not be half so much fun if he could not have generals around him with their beautiful uniforms, bright medals, and sparkling gold braid.

"Since this upside-down man is dangerous enough to kill people in their beds," the King told his generals, "he is the same thing as a weapon.

"Our guns and bombs are also dangerous," he said, "but we do not destroy them. No. We use them to kill our enemies in Isteria.

"Since this upside-down man is dangerous, it would be foolish to destroy him. Yes. We shall use him as a weapon to kill our enemies in Isteria."

The generals gazed in wonder at the King.

How smart he was, they said.

"This upside-down man," said the King, "is Delirium's secret weapon."

N EXT MORNING the royal science advisor told the King the upside-down man looked to him like the work of a mad scientist he had known in college. This mad scientist, who was named Doctor Frankenstein, had had a strange ambition, he told the King.

When asked what they wanted to do when they grew up, all the other mad scientists used to say, "I want to help people."

But Doctor Frankenstein always said, "I want to make people."

The King asked where Doctor Frankenstein might be found, and the royal science advisor said that in college he always lived in spooky old castles. "He used to say a spooky old castle was the only place for a mad scientist to live," he said.

It took the King no time at all to learn that there was a spooky old castle within three miles of his camp, and even less time to gallop there and bang on the castle door.

"I command you to make me three million of these

dangerous upside-down men by Christmas," King Zugg told Doctor Frankenstein.

He pointed to the caged upside-down man whom he had brought along for Doctor Frankenstein to copy.

"Not one day later than Christmas, mind you," said the King. "On Christmas with three million of these deadly secret weapons, I shall make a surprise attack on Isteria and kill all our enemies. Then Delirium will be the most powerful kingdom on this side of Doom Mountain, and there will be happiness for everyone forever."

Every one of the three million upside-down men must be exactly alike, the King commanded.

"If there is any bumbling," he said, "you shall be hung from the rafters of this castle workroom and lowered very slowly into tanks of boiling oil."

Doctor Frankenstein and Lazlo went to work right away. "Three million is a lot of men to make between Halloween and Christmas," Doctor Frankenstein grumbled. But the thought of being dipped in boiling oil made them work very hard.

Luckily there was an unusually terrible storm that very night with unusually terrible lightning. It was so terrible, in fact, that Lazlo was able to make one whole new man while Doctor Frankenstein was in the kitchen cooking dinner.

The upside-down man kept mooing from his cage as he watched Lazlo trying to make a copy of him. Once or twice he mooed so sadly that Lazlo wondered if he was trying to say something.

Doctor Frankenstein was still frying the potatoes when Lazlo connected the wires that would help the lightning bring his new man to life.

"CRASH!" went the thunder.

"ZZZSSPRRCRACKK!" went the lightning.

"SSSZZZZSSSZZZZTTTT!" sizzled the wires connected to the new man's body.

The castle lights went dark, then came on again, and the upside-down man mooed from his cage as if trying to tell Lazlo something important.

When sparks no longer came off the wires and no more smoke came from the nose, Lazlo looked happily at his work.

The man sat up and smiled the same beautiful smile Lazlo had first seen on the upside-down man when he was brand new.

Then—!

Then Lazlo saw that he had bumbled again.

This was not a man.

It was a girl.

Lazlo wanted to kick himself.

"What a bumbler I am!" he said.

He had meant to make a man. Where had he gone wrong? Maybe down in the cellar when he had spilled a whole tray of people parts and gotten them all mixed up.

A girl!

What was worse, she was not even an upside-down girl.

Her hands were on her wrists where hands belonged. Her feet were on her ankles where feet belonged. They were beautiful hands and feet and wrists and ankles, too.

And yet this girl seemed ugly to Lazlo.

27

How can a girl with such beautiful hands and feet and wrists and ankles be so ugly? Lazlo wondered.

The girl rose from the table and smiled at Lazlo. It was the smile of a girl who feels beautiful.

Lazlo thought she was so ugly he could not stand to look at her, and his face showed his disgust. What was wrong with her?

When the girl saw that Lazlo thought she was ugly, her smile went away. She walked to the same mirror in which the upside-down man had first looked at himself.

She saw a girl with beautiful hands and wrists and feet and ankles. But there was something about her ears that did not go with the rest of her.

"The ears!" cried Lazlo.

"I have bumbled again!"

Oh, how he wished he had gone into King Zugg's army long ago and died in battle against Isteria. That at least would have saved him from this life of bumbling.

This time Lazlo had bumbled with ears. Instead of putting in a cow's voice for the mooing, which King Zugg wanted in all his three million upside-down men, Lazlo had put on cow's ears. A huge, hairy, furry, black and white set of cow's ears. This made the poor girl look so funny that Lazlo had to laugh at her.

Seeing that she was so ugly that she made people laugh, the girl began to cry. She stood before the mirror holding her beautiful hands over the huge, hairy, furry, black and white cow's ears and cried without making a sound.

The upside-down man had seen everything from his cage. He had seen the heart Lazlo had placed in the girl, and now he remembered it. It was, he thought, the most beautiful heart he had ever seen.

He did not stop to think that it was the *only* heart he had ever seen, for he did not want to be bothered with scientific details at this moment. He wanted to help this girl with the beautiful heart.

"Moo," he said gently.

"Moo, moo, moo, moo."

The mooing made no sense to Lazlo. "If you've heard one moo, you've heard them all," he always said.

The girl understood, however.

At the first moo her cow ears stood straight up.

"If you cry like that," the upside-down man was saying, "you will break your beautiful heart."

"Beautiful!" said the girl, still crying. "How can I be beautiful if people laugh when they look at me?"

The upside-down man made a long speech. To Lazlo it sounded like a lot of dull mooing, but the girl with the cow ears understood every word.

"What people have on their heads does not make them beautiful or ugly," the upside-down man said. "It is

29

what people have inside them that makes them beautiful or makes them ugly. And you have the most beautiful heart I have ever seen."

"I don't believe it," the girl said, although she had stopped crying. "No one who was truly beautiful inside could have such huge, furry, hairy black and white ears as mine."

"Oh, you are wrong!" said the upside-down man.

"Because of your beautiful heart you are able to hear those who are miserable and cry out for comfort. What good are lovely ears if they cannot hear the cries of people who need help? Your ears, lovely girl, are the most beautiful ears anyone can ever have because they help you hear in your beautiful heart."

Lazlo was alarmed by this strange talk, half of which he did not understand, and he ran to get Doctor Frankenstein.

"I am the one who is ugly," said the upside-down man.

"What a terrible thing to say about yourself," the girl protested.

"It is true," the upside-down man insisted. "I am so ugly that people wanted to kill me until the King saved me. And the King saved me only because he thought me so ugly I could be used to kill his enemies."

"What a terrible king he must be!" cried the girl.

The upside-down man said that three million copies of him were being made and would be used to destroy the kingdom of Isteria on Christmas Day.

"You poor thing," said the girl. "We must get you out of that cage. Isn't there a village nearby where we can get help?"

"It is useless," said the upside-down man. "If the villagers see me they will kill me for being ugly. If I escape and the King catches me again, he will have me dipped in boiling oil for running away with his secret weapon."

"What is his secret weapon?" she asked.

"Me," said the upside-down man.

Just then Doctor Frankenstein ran into the workroom with Lazlo. When he saw the girl his jaw fell open and he roared with laughter.

"That girl—" he began, before his laughter drowned his words.

"That girl—." Again he could not speak because he was laughing so hard.

"That girl," he finally said, "is the ugliest girl I have ever seen in my life."

And he laughed, and laughed, and laughed, and laughed. And Lazlo laughed with him.

At this the girl forgot about her beautiful heart and burst into tears and ran from the room.

"Don't run away!" the upside-down man mooed.

"Please don't! Without you I am all alone with no one to hear me!"

But the girl did not hear him now.

She ran from the castle. Crying so hard that it is a wonder she did not break her beautiful heart, she ran down the side of Doom Mountain while the lightning flashed about her and the thunder roared.

Running to telephone the police to look out for a very ugly girl, Doctor Frankenstein saw the key to the upside-down man's cage lying on the workroom floor.

"Lazlo," he said, "be sure to put that key where the upside-down man can't reach it." And out he went.

It took Lazlo only ten minutes to bumble again.

"There is that key," he said to himself. "Now what was it Doctor Frankenstein asked me to do with that key?

"Oh, yes, I remember. Be sure to put the key where the upside-down man can reach it."

And this is exactly what Lazlo did before going to the cellar to start working on another man.

Unlocking his cage, the upside-down man ran out of

the castle and raced as fast as he could to catch up with the girl with the beautiful heart.

If she reached the village, he feared, the people would laugh at her ears until she cried so desperately that her beautiful heart would break.

It did not matter to him now that the villagers would kill him if they saw him, for if the girl's beautiful heart were broken he would be dead for the rest of his life.

When he reached the village all the streets were dark and wet. The only light came from the inn. Inside there was loud laughter.

Looking in the window, he saw the girl surrounded by a laughing circle of men and women pointing at her huge, hairy, furry, black and white ears.

The upside-down man was too late.

"Has anybody ever seen an uglier girl anywhere in the world?" cried the man with a fat barrel of a stomach and long rickety legs thin as beanpoles and the huge wrinkled nose that was as red as a tomato and almost as big.

"She is so ugly she will drive my customers away!" yelled the innkeeper. With his broom he whacked her on her ears and chased her into the night.

As she ran sobbing past the upside-down man he mooed to her, but she did not hear.

Ah, he thought. *Surely her heart is broken, for she can no longer hear me.*

She ran past the fountain that splashed dirty water and towards the stream where the fish were dying.

The upside-down man ran after her, and saw that she was going to drown herself. Again he mooed for her to wait, but she did not hear.

"Surely they have broken her beautiful heart," he said, "and she will never hear me again."

He mooed once more. It was the saddest moo he had ever made.

"I need you," it said. "If you die with your beautiful heart, I shall die, too. It will not matter that the King will use me to kill others, for with no one left whose heart can hear me, I shall be dead of loneliness and despair."

The girl turned from the bank of the stream and walked to the upside-down man.

She bent down and kissed him softly on the cheek and then took him by the hand.

"You shall never become one of the King's weapons," she said, "for in this terrible kingdom of Delirium where birds never sing and fish die in the streams and the sky is dark at noon, you have the power to make the broken-hearted wish to go on living."

His happiness filled him from hand to toe, and as they walked along the edge of the mountain he told her of another kingdom he had heard about.

While caged in the King's camp, he had heard two

soldiers talking. They spoke of a strange kingdom on the far side of Doom Mountain. It was a kingdom where nobody from Delirium ever went because it was so unfriendly to Delirium's way of life.

It was a kingdom of sunshine and crystal-bright air. Its streams were alive with fish, and its fountains ran pure, cool water.

Bluebirds sang in the sunlight, giant butterflies sat on the cornflowers in the morning, and at night there were nightingales which sang the people to sleep.

It was called the Kingdom of Serenity, the soldiers said. The people of Delirium would feel so miserable there, they said, that King Zugg did not even want to conquer it.

When the upside-down man had told the girl all this, she said they should climb to the top of Doom Mountain and look for this strange kingdom on the far side.

They had climbed half the night and almost reached the top of Doom Mountain where the dark is darkest, when the upside-down man thought of Lazlo.

"We must go back," he said, "and get the boy, and take him with us, or else he will come to a terrible end."

"That awful bumbler?" asked the girl.

"He is just a boy."

"But look at the mess he made of us," the girl said.

"No, you are wrong," the upside-down man said. "If it had not been for his bumbling we would be just like the people of Delirium. It was his bumbling that has made it possible for us to be beautiful."

The girl heard her beautiful heart speak and knew that Lazlo needed her.

"You are right," she said to the upside-down man. "We must help the boy."

Back they turned and headed down the side of Doom Mountain toward Doctor Frankenstein's castle.

WHILE THE UPSIDE-DOWN MAN and the girl were still high up on Doom Mountain, King Zugg called on Doctor Frankenstein to see how the work was going.

When he found the upside-down man gone, the King flew into such a rage that he beat the castle's stone walls with his sword.

When he heard about the girl with the cow ears who had led the upside-down man away, the King kicked the stone steps so hard that he broke the steel toes of his armor.

"Thanks to you two bumblers," he told Lazlo and

Doctor Frankenstein, "Delirium has lost the secret weapon that would have killed everybody in Isteria before Christmas dinner."

The girl with cow ears, he said, was probably a spy from Isteria who had stolen his secret weapon. The very thought made the King so furious he struck the stone walls with his great battle axe.

Calling his generals and colonels and majors and captains and lieutenants and sergeant-majors into the castle workroom, he ordered Doctor Frankenstein and Lazlo hung by their thumbs from the rafters.

Then he ordered tanks of boiling oil brought into the room and placed where the Doctor and Lazlo could be slowly lowered into them.

Hanging thumbs-up from a rafter over a huge tank of oil that had started to bubble, Lazlo looked at Doctor Frankenstein.

"Do you, as a mad scientist, have any ideas for cooling off that boiling oil?" he asked.

"You bumbler!" said the Doctor. "We wouldn't be in this mess if it weren't for you. If I could get my hands on a broom I'd beat you black and blue."

"I try to do things right," Lazlo said. "All I want is to be as helpful to people as I possibly can."

Down below on the floor the King was storming

around the room kicking his generals, who then kicked his colonels, who then kicked his majors, who then kicked his captains, who then kicked his lieutenants, who then kicked his sergeant-majors.

After that the King began breaking up the furniture.

"Isn't that boiling oil hot enough yet?" he cried.

"If the King isn't careful," Lazlo said to Doctor Frankenstein, "he is going to hit the red button accidentally and get himself into trouble."

"A fat lot I care!" said the mad scientist.

But Lazlo cared. He liked to be helpful to people, and thought it his special duty to be helpful to the King.

"Your Majesty!" he called down from the rafters. "Your Majesty!"

"What is it, bungler?" asked the enraged King Zugg.

"Whatever you do, your Majesty," said Lazlo, "remember not to push that red button."

"Bother your silly red buttons!" cried the King, at the same time smashing the red button a terrible smash with his battle axe.

Instantly, the castle floor opened beneath him. It was a cold murderous dank yawn. Before the King could draw another breath, down he slid.

Down into the pit.

Down, down, down.

Down into the endless inky-black night trailing shrieks and howls that sounded miles and miles away before a tiny splash told Lazlo that King Zugg the Third had gone forever.

Behind him slid his generals, and then his colonels, and then his majors, and then his captains, and then his lieutenants, and then his sergeant-majors. Each went with a long shriek and a fading howl and a final tiny splash in distant black water.

And behind them all tumbled the two great bubbling tanks of boiling oil.

At last there was absolute quiet. An oily steam rose from the gaping pit.

Lazlo peered down into the bottomless hole and felt thankful that the King's men could tie such tight knots around something as slippery as thumbs.

"Gosh, Doctor," Lazlo said to the hanging mad scientist, "the King was one of the worst bumblers I ever saw."

AFTER A SHORT WHILE the upside-down man poked his legs through the workroom door and saw what had happened.

Doctor Frankenstein directed him to a secret button that closed the floor again, and when the upside-down man had done this he climbed to the rafters and cut down Lazlo.

"I don't suppose you would consider getting me down from here, too," Doctor Frankenstein said.

The upside-down man mooed.

"I didn't think so," said the Doctor.

The upside-down man had the girl tell Lazlo that they were going to cross over Doom Mountain and live in the strange kingdom of Serenity.

"We shall take you with us, if you wish to go, for you are even more unfit than we to live in the kingdom of Delirium," the girl told Lazlo.

"You are right about that," Lazlo said. "If I stay here I'm sure to end up boiled in oil before my next birthday."

The three of them left the castle for the last time and made the hard climb up Doom Mountain.

It was dawn when they crossed into the kingdom of Serenity. The sky was clear and a flight of swallows sang them down the warm mountainside into a meadow that was blooming with golden morning.

How Doctor Frankenstein ever got down from his rafter I do not know, but I am sure he did. These mad scientists are clever.

In any case, not long ago a man calling himself Doctor Frankenstein tried to cross the border into the kingdom of Serenity. The guards refused to let him enter.

In Serenity there is a law against letting mad scientists enter the kingdom. This is because mad scientists believe it is scientifically impossible for people to live happily ever after.

If such gloomy ideas were spread in the kingdom, it is feared, the birds might stop singing, which would disturb the many, many people who are living happily ever after there at this very moment, including the upside-down man, the girl with the beautiful heart, and Lazlo the bumbling boy.